OXFORD VOCAL MUSIC

Ralph Vaughan Williams

THREE VOCALISES

For Soprano and B♭ Clarinet

OXFORD
UNIVERSITY PRESS

THREE VOCALISES
for Soprano Voice and Clarinet

R. VAUGHAN WILLIAMS
(1958)

I PRELUDE

It is probable that the composer would have added more dynamic indications had he been able to make final revisions before publication. It has been decided that dynamics should be printed as they appear in the manuscript.

Three Vocalises

II SCHERZO

Three Vocalises

III QUASI MENUETTO

Three Vocalises

OXFORD UNIVERSITY PRESS

OXFORD
UNIVERSITY PRESS

www.oup.com

ISBN 978-0-19-385027-9

9 780193 850279